Henry Cole

Principal Tate Is Running Late!

Katherine Tegen Books
An Imprint of HarperCollinsPublishers

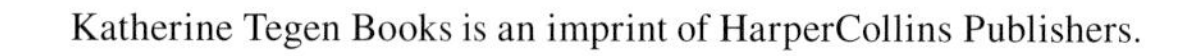

Katherine Tegen Books is an imprint of HarperCollins Publishers.

Principal Tate Is Running Late!

www.harpercollinschildrens.com

ISBN 978-0-06-302574-5

The artist used watercolors and ink to create the illustrations for this book.
Typography by Dana Fritts
21 22 23 24 25 RTLO 10 9 8 7 6 5 4 3 2 1
❖
First Edition

For Susan Phillips,
Principal Extraordinaire

HARDY COUNTY SCHOOL
SCHOOL BUS

The school day had started.
All systems go!
Buses brought cargo . . . ready to grow.

The one in command was
Principal Tate.
Hardy School was first-rate
because Tate was so great.

She guided each student
to try to be better.
To be a goal-setter . . . and a go-getter!

To keep apple-pie order, it was always Tate's way
to cheerlead each day and make things A-OK.

Tate helped fire drills go smoothly
and helped meetings run well,

from morning's first bell
to dismissal's farewell.

But that morning, Ms. Dee . . .
ordinarily unfazed . . .
noticed, amazed,
Tate's blinds still unraised!

Here it was, a quarter ’til eight,

and Principal Tate
was running late!

Outside in the hallway,
two youngsters were brawling:
one loudly bawling, the other name-calling.

And a new kid threw up . . .
(It *was* her first day.)
And one kid named Trey
wore his undies wrong way.

Then two visitors came:
a computer technician
and a bigwig clinician
who was a state dietitian.

Outside of Tate's office,
parents were grouchy,
looking quite touchy,
lined up on Tate's couchy.

"We have appointments!" one of them whined.

But Principal Tate was running behind!

"Uh-oh," said Ms. Dee. "This isn't like Tate!
To make people wait? That's something she'd hate!"

Then, at 8:17, one kid, almost dizzy,
had a hissy fit tizzy ’cause his hair was too frizzy.

Then *more* visitors came
and formed a long queue.
And a fire drill was due . . . at 8:52!

The school board arrived for its bimonthly meeting.
Plus the guys completing their check on the heating.

But where was our Tate? wondered Ms. Dee.
Her space, she could see, out in front, was still free.

"Attention," Dee announced, to all those at Hardy.
"The latest is this: Mrs. Tate's running tardy!"

But the staff and the students . . .
all Hardy crew . . .
they knew what to do and how to pull through.

Mrs. Clem, the art teacher,
led those parents away.
They had a field day,
with hands full of clay.

Mrs. Chan and her chorus
played the Hardy school song
and got the school board, and the techie,
to sing right along.

Frank, the custodian, cleaned up the mess.
The nurse, Mr. Kress, got Trey to re-dress.

The guest dietitian,
who was awed by Ms. Price,
had burritos and rice . . .
not one time, but twice.

Mrs. Lee and two friends,
they quickly got busy
finding how-tos for Izzie,
the one looking frizzy.

And Ms. Dee, in the office, was planning ahead.
"The fire drill," she said, "is tomorrow instead."

But it was Mr. Morales
who deserved an A-plus.
He pulled up with no fuss . . .
and with Tate in his bus!

Everyone smiled when, at the front gate,
came Principal Tate, just a teensy bit late!

Tate was so proud, she practically glowed!
Despite being slowed
on the side of the road.

She grinned ear to ear.
The day had worked out!
Tate wanted to shout that she never had doubt!

When a school gets along,
it's a place of community,
working so beautifully, together in unity.